The Boxcar Children Mysteries

THE BOX THAT WATCH FOUND

created by
GERTRUDE CHANDLER WARNER

Illustrated by Robert Papp

ALBERT WHITMAN & Company
Morton Grove, IL

The Box That Watch Found
Created by Gertrude Chandler Warner;
Illustrated by Robert Papp.

ISBN 13: 978-0-8075-5568-2 (hardcover)
ISBN 13: 978-0-8075-5569-9 (paperback)

Cover art by Robert Papp.

For information about Albert Whitman & Company,
visit our web site at www.albertwhitman.com.

Contents

THE BOX THAT WATCH FOUND

CHAPTER 1

The Strange Box

"Whoa! Slow down, Watch!" six-year-old Benny Alden cried as he held tight to his dog's leash. "I can't run that fast!"

Benny's eight-year-old sister, Violet, laughed. "I don't think Watch can slow down, Benny. He's too excited!"

"That's because he knows we're going to the dog park," twelve-year-old Jessie said.

It looked like the girls were right. Watch's tongue lolled to the side of his mouth as he led the children up the hill. If dogs could smile, Watch was definitely smiling. But poor Benny could hardly keep up with him.

Fourteen-year-old Henry trotted up alongside his younger brother. A Frisbee dangled from one hand. "Do you want me to take Watch for you, Benny?"

"No," Benny said, huffing and puffing. He gripped the leash so tight his knuckles were turning white. "I've got him."

"Are you sure?" Jessie asked as she and Violet ran up behind Henry.

"Yes," Benny said. "We're almost there." They could hear dogs yipping and barking in the distance.

A few minutes later, the Aldens entered a large fenced-in area that was bordered by woods. A sign on the fence read: *Welcome to Greenfield Dog Park.*

"Sit, Watch!" Benny commanded.

Watch let out a little whimper. He clearly wanted to run and play with the other dogs. But he sat right there on the path. His tail swished the dirt from side to side.

Watch had been with the Aldens since their

days of living in the boxcar. Their parents had just died and the children were supposed to go and live with their grandfather, James Alden. But they didn't know him. They were afraid he'd be mean. So they ran away and lived in an abandoned boxcar in the woods. Watch joined them soon after that.

Eventually, their grandfather found the children in the woods and took them to live with him. He let Watch come, too. The children found out Grandfather wasn't mean at all. In fact, he was so nice that he even had the boxcar moved to his backyard so they could play in it anytime they wanted to.

Benny unsnapped Watch's leash, then put it in his pocket. "Okay, boy," he said cheerfully. "You're free!"

That was all Watch needed. He dashed off toward a tall white poodle.

"Hey, that poodle looks a lot like Chester," Violet said, shading her eyes.

Chester was a dog that belonged to their grandfather's longtime friend, Cal Edwards. Cal ran the Greenfield Nature Center, which was located on the other side of the woods. He was also the person Grandfather called when he needed help fixing something.

"I think that *is* Chester," Henry said as he watched the poodle and Watch nuzzle noses.

"If Chester's here, then Cal must be here, too," Jessie said.

"There he is!" Benny pointed at a man who was just walking from behind a tree. He carried a large black garbage bag in one hand and a small red ball in the other.

Henry waved to him. "Hello, Cal," he called. The children hurried toward him.

Cal smiled. "Well, hello there!" he called back. "When I saw Watch, I figured you kids and James had to be here, too."

"Grandfather's not here," Violet said. "He had a meeting this afternoon."

"That's too bad," Cal said. "It's a beautiful day for the dog park."

"Yes, it is," Jessie agreed. The others nodded.

Chester nuzzled the ball in Cal's hand and

Cal threw it as far as he could. Both Chester and Watch bolted after it.

"It's nice that your job is so close that you can come to the dog park with Chester," Henry said.

"It sure is," said Cal. "We just cut through those woods over there. It takes us only a few minutes."

"You must pick up lots of garbage on your way," Benny said.

"What makes you say that, Benny?" Cal asked with surprise.

"Because you have such a big garbage bag," Benny replied.

"Oh, this?" Cal said, lifting the big black bag. "This isn't garbage. It's—" But before Cal could explain what was in the bag, his cell phone rang.

"Excuse me," he said. He reached into his front pocket and pulled out his phone. He flipped it open and put it to his ear. "Hello? Yes, this is Cal." A look of concern flashed across his face. "Just a minute, please."

Cal covered his phone with his hand and

turned to the Aldens. "I'm sorry, kids, but I need to take this call. I'll see you all later."

Cal whistled for his dog, who came bounding over. Cal continued his telephone conversation while he walked. The children waved good-bye as Cal and his dog walked back toward the nature center.

"Anyone want to play Frisbee?" Henry asked, holding the Frisbee up in the air.

"Sure," Jessie said.

They walked to the edge of the park, away from most of the other dogs, and Henry threw the disk to Jessie. Jessie threw it to Benny and Benny jumped as the Frisbee sailed over his head. But he couldn't jump high enough. The Frisbee landed in the grass behind him.

"Sorry, Benny," Jessie called.

"That's okay," Benny said. He and Watch raced to the fallen Frisbee and Watch barked eagerly when Benny stooped to pick it up.

"Do you want to try and catch it, Watch?" Benny asked the dog. The children had been trying to teach Watch to jump up and catch the Frisbee in his mouth.

Benny pulled his arm back and let the Frisbee go as hard as he could. The Frisbee wobbled in the air, bounced twice on the ground, then rolled until it hit the fence.

But Watch didn't mind. He ran after it, his tail wagging.

"Cheer up, Benny," Jessie said. "You'll get the hang of throwing a Frisbee."

"Watch me, Benny," Violet said as she took the Frisbee from Watch. "You have to sort of flick your wrist like this." She let the Frisbee go, then watched in horror as it sailed over the fence and into the woods.

"Oh, no," Violet said, clasping her hands to her cheeks. "I didn't mean to throw it out of the dog park!"

"That's okay, Violet," Jessie said. "We'll just go and get it." She pushed on the gate and Watch squeezed through the opening before she could hold him back. He plowed ahead of them into the woods.

"Uh-oh," Benny said. "Shouldn't Watch be on a leash when he's not in the dog park?" He pulled Watch's leash out of his pocket.

"I'll get him," Henry said. "He's just going after the Frisbee. I'll put his leash on and we'll go right back to the park as soon as we find it."

The children hurried into the woods. They found the Frisbee just a few feet in, but they didn't see Watch anywhere.

"Where is Watch?" Violet asked, turning her head from side to side.

Henry leaned over to pick up the Frisbee. "I don't know," he said.

They were on a dirt path that was covered with pine needles. Trees and bushes grew all around them.

"He wasn't that far ahead of us," Jessie said.

"Yeah, but he runs fast," Benny said, growing worried. "And he might have chased a squirrel or something off the path."

"Don't worry, Benny," Jessie said. "We'll find him." She put her hands around her mouth and called, "Watch! Here, boy!"

They heard a short bark in response. It came from a cluster of trees off to the right.

"There he is," Violet said with relief. They all hurried over to him. Benny snapped the leash to Watch's collar.

Watch stood on his back legs, digging at something in a pile of brush between two trees. He hardly paid any attention to the children. He was more interested in whatever was in the middle of the brush.

"Hey, he's got something!" Benny said as Watch uncovered a square metal object in the brush.

"What is it?" Jessie asked.

"I don't know," Henry said.

All four of them brushed the sticks and leaves away from the metal object and Henry lifted it out. "It's a box of some kind," he said. The box had some black lettering on the outside. "Official Geocache," it read.

"Geo . . . geo . . . " Benny tried to sound the word out, then gave up. "What's that word, Henry?"

"I think it's pronounced 'geo-cash,'" Henry said.

"Geocache?" Violet asked. "What's that?"

"I don't know," Henry said. "I know *cache* means hiding place. But I don't know what geocache means."

"Since it's pronounced geo-cash, maybe it means there's money hidden in there?" Benny said.

"Maybe," Violet said.

"Well, there's only one way to find out," Jessie said. "Let's open it up and see what's inside!"

CHAPTER 2

It's Called Geocaching!

"It's just a box full of plastic bags," Violet said when Henry opened the metal box.

"No money?" Benny asked. He stood on his tiptoes so he could see inside the box.

"No money," Henry said. "But it looks like there are things inside the bags."

"What kind of things?" Jessie asked.

There were so many small bags stuffed inside the box that it was hard to see what was inside any of them. But Henry managed

12

to pull a couple out.

"There's a notebook and pencil in one," Henry said, holding it up. "And a stuffed armadillo in this other one."

"Oh, he's cute!" Violet said, taking the armadillo from Henry.

"I see a toothbrush in the bottom of the box," Jessie said, peering inside.

"A toothbrush?" Violet laughed.

"Oh, and look!" Jessie reached in and grabbed another bag. This one had two copper-colored coins in it. "There *is* money in here. But it's not American money."

Benny opened the bag and pulled out one of the coins. "It says 'one peso,'" he read.

"That's Mexican money," Henry said.

"It's kind of hard to look at all this stuff out here in the woods," Jessie said, giving Watch a pat on the head. "Maybe we should bring the box home so we can get a better look at it."

"Good idea, Jessie," Violet said.

The children stuffed the bags back inside the box and closed it up. Henry picked up the box and the children started to leave.

But as they were walking away, they heard a voice call out, "Hey, you kids. What do you think you're doing? Where are you going with that box?"

They turned and saw a man in a red jacket walking over from the nature center. He was tall with short dark hair that circled a bald spot. A dark-haired boy around Henry's age hurried along beside him.

"I didn't mean to scare you," the man said in a friendlier voice as he and the boy came closer. They both smiled at the Aldens. "I just wanted to make sure you're not taking that box with you."

The Aldens glanced at each other.

"Well, actually," Henry began. "We were planning to take it with us."

"We found it in that pile of brush over there," Benny said, pointing behind him.

"Is it yours?" Violet asked.

"Not ours, exactly," the dark-haired boy said. "You might say it belongs to everybody."

"Everybody?" Jessie asked. "What do you mean?"

"Let me explain," the man said. "I'm Ned Robertson, by the way. And this is my son, Andy."

The Aldens introduced themselves and Watch, then Mr. Robertson asked, "Have you ever heard of geocaching?"

"You mean like it says on the box?" Violet asked.

"Yes," Mr. Robertson replied.

"No. What is geocaching?" Henry asked.

"It's a kind of treasure hunt," Mr. Robertson explained. "Do you know what this is?" He held out the small yellow gadget in his hand. It had black buttons on the sides and a screen in the middle.

The children shook their heads.

"It's a global positioning system—GPS for short," Mr. Robertson said. "It shows you where you are on the planet. If you're out in the woods, you can use it to help you find your way so you don't get lost."

"I've read about those," Henry said. "They use radio signals from satellites to pinpoint where you are, don't they?"

"That's exactly right," Mr. Robertson said.

"Cool!" Benny said.

"And," Andy continued. "If you're into geocaching like my dad and me, you can use a GPS to help you find a hidden treasure box."

"How?" Jessie asked.

"Well, there's a website that lists all the caches in the world," Mr. Robertson said. "It's at www.geocaching.com. You can go to that website and enter in a zip code. That'll show you all the caches that are in or near that zip code."

"There are more than seventy-five of them hidden within about ten miles of here," Andy said.

"Really?" Benny's eyes grew wide.

"Yes." Mr. Robertson smiled at Benny. "They're all listed on the website. And they all have names. For instance, this one that you stumbled upon is called 'Walk in the Woods.' If you want to try and find a certain cache, all you have to do is hook your GPS up to your computer, then enter the waypoint that's listed there on the site—"

"A waypoint?" Violet asked.

"It's a way of marking a particular spot on the earth. In this case, it marks where a cache is hidden. Once you enter the waypoint into your GPS, the GPS will help you find it," Mr. Robertson said.

"You still have to look around for the cache, though," Andy said. "A GPS doesn't tell you exactly *where* it is. It tells you which direction to go and how far away you are from it. See?"

He held the GPS so the Aldens could see the screen. An arrow in the middle of the screen pointed behind them. And the distance above the arrow read 102 feet.

"Why does it say we're 102 feet from the box?" Jessie asked. "It's right here!" She tapped the box in Henry's hands. The Robertsons' GPS couldn't have been more than 7 feet from Henry.

"The GPS doesn't know the cache is here, in Henry's hands," Andy said. "It'll take you to the spot where the box was originally hidden. If it's been moved, you're out of luck. You won't find it. That's why it's so important to put the cache back exactly where you found it. So other people can find it after you."

"We'll put it back right now," Henry said, turning around. The others followed him back to the pile of brush.

"Before you put it back, you might want to sign the log book," Mr. Robertson said.

"Log book?" Violet said.

"Yes. Every cache has one," said Mr. Robertson. "You choose a nickname for yourself and then you sign the log book. You can write about your adventure finding the cache on the website, too, especially if there's something wrong with the cache or if something interesting happened to you while you were looking for it."

"But we weren't looking for it," Benny said. "We just found it!"

"Then you can write that, too," Mr. Robertson said, laughing.

"And you can always take something out

of the box if you leave something else in its place," Andy said.

"There's never anything very valuable in the containers," Mr. Robertson said. "People don't do this to try to get rich. They do it because it's fun to see whether they can find a hidden treasure with a GPS."

Henry leaned against a fallen tree and opened up the box again. "I remember seeing a notebook in here," he said, pulling out the plastic bag with the small blue notebook. He opened it to the first page. "Hey, it says here, 'Geocache site. Please read. Congratulations! You've found it.' And then it goes on to explain everything Mr. Robertson and Andy just told us."

"If we had only looked in the log book, we'd have known all this and we wouldn't have taken the box," Jessie said.

"That's okay," Mr. Robertson said. "I'm sure you kids would've brought it back as soon as you realized what it was."

Henry flipped through the pages in the notebook until he came to a blank sheet. "So, we're supposed to write something in this book?" he asked.

"Yes," Andy said. "You might want to say that this is your first find."

"And you can make up an interesting nickname for yourselves," Mr. Robertson added. "For instance, when Andy and I sign a log book, we call ourselves the Trailblazers."

"What nickname should we use?" Henry asked.

"I've got an idea," Benny cried. "How about the Boxcar Kids?"

"The Boxcar Kids?" Andy said. "What does that mean?"

The Aldens explained about their boxcar.

"I like it," Violet said. "Let's call ourselves the Boxcar Kids."

"Yes, let's!" Jessie put in.

Henry wrote, *This was the first cache we ever found. We found it by accident. We're looking forward to more geocaching!*

"Do you want to take anything?" Mr. Robertson asked.

"I don't know." Jessie scratched her head.

"We don't have anything to put in there, do we?"

The Aldens checked their pockets. Nobody had anything to leave in the box.

"We always carry a few trinkets for geocaching," Andy said. He pulled a little wind-up frog out of his inside jacket pocket. "If you want to take something, you could leave this in its place."

"That's nice of you," Violet said.

"Go on," Mr. Robertson urged. "Pick something. You have to take something to remember your first find."

"Hmm. What should we take?" Henry asked the others.

"Take the coins! Take the coins!" Benny cried, jumping up and down.

Henry pulled out the bag with the coins and handed it to Benny. Then he wrote: *took coins, left frog.*

"You should sign the log, too," Henry said, handing the notebook to Mr. Robertson. "You would've found the box if we hadn't. Plus you gave us the frog."

"Okay," Mr. Robertson said. "I'll say that the Trailblazers were here with the Boxcar Kids." He smiled as he jotted a few lines in the notebook. When he finished writing, he sealed the notebook back up in the plastic bag, put it in the box, and closed it. Then the Aldens and the Robertsons buried the box back in the brush between the two trees just the way they'd found it.

"There's supposed to be another cache not too far from here," Andy said. "It's called 'Edge of the Forest.' Do you want to come with us and see if we can find it?"

"Sure," the Aldens replied eagerly.

"Let me tell the GPS we're looking for a different cache now," Mr. Robertson said, pressing the button on the side of the gadget a few times. "Okay, now we're set up to find the 'Edge of the Forest' cache."

Mr. Robertson handed the GPS to Benny, then said, "Which way do we want to go?"

Benny peered at the arrow on the screen. "That way," he said, pointing deeper into the woods.

"I wonder if it's over by the nature center?" Violet said. "If we stay on this trail, we'll come out over there."

"Could be," Mr. Robertson said. "I think we're probably about half a mile from the nature center."

The group walked single file in a line behind Benny. Jessie held Watch's leash. Watch sniffed the ground as they walked.

After a little while, Benny said, "It's 52 feet over this way!" He pointed to the right. The path curved to the left.

They were almost through the woods at this point. They could see the nature center building just ahead.

"We must be close then," Andy said. "Start looking, everyone. Check tree stumps, holes in trees, piles of brush, anything that looks like it could hold a medium-sized container."

"The GPS is going crazy!" Benny cried. "The arrow is turning round and round. And the number keeps changing from 13 to 20 to 15 to 17—"

"That means it's right around here," Mr. Robertson said.

The Aldens and the Robertsons lifted small logs and peered in hollows of trees.

Finally, Jessie said, "I think I found it!" She pulled a plastic storage container out from between two logs. This one was smaller than the first cache. It contained a yo-yo, a plastic watch, two keychains, and another notebook and pencil.

"Hooray!" Benny jumped up and down. "This is fun!"

"You know, there's a geocaching club here in Greenfield," Mr. Robertson said. "We meet at the nature center. Maybe you'd like to check out one of our meetings? You might even be able to borrow a GPS from the club if you want to do some more geocaching on your own."

"Can we?" Benny asked his brother and sisters.

"Sure," Henry said. "Do you know when the next meeting is?"

"I think we're meeting this Friday at

noon," Mr. Robertson replied. "But check the website to be sure."

"We will," Jessie said. "Thanks for teaching us about geocaching!"

"It was our pleasure," Mr. Robertson said.

"See you on Friday!" Henry said.

"I wonder what we'll find the next time we go geocaching," Violet said.

"Maybe we'll find a mystery!" Benny said.

"Oh, Benny," Jessie laughed. "We don't find mysteries everywhere we go."

"No, but a lot of times *they* find *us*," Benny said.

CHAPTER 3

Treasure Found and Lost

"All you have to do is enter a zip code and the website will show you all the caches that are nearby," Violet told Grandfather and their housekeeper, Mrs. MacGregor, that evening.

The children had spent some time exploring www.geocaching.com. They had tried to tell Grandfather and Mrs. MacGregor what geocaching was during dinner, but everyone agreed it would be easier if the children could show them. So after dinner they all gathered

27

around the computer. Jessie sat at the keyboard and Watch curled up at her feet.

Mrs. MacGregor squinted at the screen. "All of those are names of . . . what did you call them? Caches?"

"Yes," Jessie said. "A cache is a sort of treasure box. And look." She pointed at a number on the screen. "This tells us how far away each cache is from our house."

"These two, 'Walk in the Woods' and 'Edge of the Forest' are the ones we found today," Henry said. "You can read what we wrote here."

"But if you wrote in the notebook that you found the box, why do you need to go to the website and write it again?" Grandfather asked.

"You don't have to," Jessie said. "But it's fun to read about the cache *before* you try to find it."

"And if there's something wrong with the cache, if it's missing or damaged in some way, you can let people know that by leaving a comment on the website," Henry said.

"This is all very interesting," Mrs. Mac-Gregor said, peering over Jessie's shoulder.

"All we need is a GPS unit and we can go geocaching on our own," Henry said. "Mr. Robertson told us the local geocaching club has a few to lend to new members."

"Hmm," Grandfather said. "I believe I have a little handheld GPS."

"You do?" Benny asked.

"Yes. I bought it a couple of months ago," Grandfather said. "I thought it would be useful for hiking."

"Could we see your GPS, Grandfather?" Henry asked.

"I'll go get it." Grandfather got up and went to the closet. He came back with a small canvas case that looked like a camera bag. Grandfather unzipped the case and pulled out a rectangular object with buttons and a screen.

"Hey, that looks just like the Robertsons' GPS!" Benny cried.

"Do you have a cable to hook it up to the computer?" Jessie asked.

Grandfather reached inside the case and pulled out a black cord. "I'll bet that's what this is," he said, holding it up. "I think there are some instructions in here, too." He looked inside the case again and pulled out a sheet of paper.

"Looks easy enough to set up," Henry said, looking over the instructions.

"Can we borrow your GPS for geocaching?" Violet asked.

"Sure," Grandfather said.

"Can we go geocaching tomorrow?" Benny asked.

"I don't see why not," Grandfather said.

So the children got everything set up. Then they decided which caches they wanted to try and find next.

" 'Squires Point,' " Jessie read the name of one of the caches in the list. "Isn't that the name of one of the hiking trails in the Pine Ridge Recreation Area?"

"I think it is," Henry said.

"Then I'll bet the cache is hidden somewhere around that trail," Violet said.

"I wonder if there are other caches hidden in the same area," Jessie said. "If we go out to Pine Ridge, maybe we can find several caches at the same time." She glanced up at the computer screen, then clicked on "find other caches nearby."

The Aldens downloaded the information into Grandfather's GPS. And the next day, after a good hearty breakfast, the children loaded up their pockets with small trinkets for trading and set out for the Pine Ridge Recreation Area on their bikes.

They locked their bikes to the bike rack in the gravel parking lot, then Henry got out the GPS. He turned it on and set it to find the Squires Point cache.

"It says the cache is four-tenths of a mile north of here," Henry said.

The Aldens turned toward the north. They saw a dirt trail at the edge of the parking lot. A brown sign read, *Squires Point Trail.*

"That's it!" Benny cried. "Come on, everybody. It's down that trail!"

The Aldens started down the Squires Point

Trail. Benny carried the GPS.

"I don't know if we want to stay on the trail," Benny said when the path curved to the left. "The arrow is pointing straight into those trees."

"How far are we from the cache?" Jessie asked.

"It says .14 miles," Violet read over Benny's shoulder.

"Then let's stay on the trail for now," Jessie said. "This trail curves a lot. I'll bet in a little while the GPS will be pointing straight ahead again."

So they stayed on the trail. And sure enough, after a little while the trail curved back the opposite direction.

"How far are we now?" Henry asked.

"We're 133 feet away," Benny said. "And it's straight ahead."

The Aldens kept walking. The path curved again toward the lake, but this time the Aldens followed the GPS and walked off the path.

"The GPS says it's 82 feet straight ahead,"

Benny said as they made their way through the brush. Dried leaves crunched beneath their feet. "Now it's 67 feet . . . 42 feet . . . 30 feet."

They could see the lake through the trees.

"It's got to be around here somewhere," Henry said, looking around.

They checked logs, tree hollows, piles of brush, the same sorts of places they'd found the Walk in the Woods and Edge of the Forest caches.

But they weren't able to find the Squires Point cache.

"It's not here," Benny said sadly as he sat down on a log. They'd been searching for fifteen minutes.

"Maybe this one is harder to find," Violet said.

"Why don't we look for another one nearby," Jessie suggested.

"There's supposed to be one called 'Muffy's Hideaway' right around here, too. It's over that way." Henry pointed back the way they'd come. "Let's see if we have better luck

finding that one."

So the Aldens set the GPS to find Muffy's Hideaway. Then they turned around and headed back to the path. As they walked, they watched the numbers on the GPS get smaller and smaller.

"It's probably over here," Jessie said, leading the way to a stand of trees.

The children searched every tree and rock in the area. But once again they came up empty.

"It's not as much fun when we don't find the caches," Benny grumbled.

"There's one more we can look for," Henry said. "I think the 'Chipmunk Challenge' cache is going to be down that other trail across the parking lot from where we parked our bikes."

The children tromped back to the parking lot, then crossed over to another dirt trail.

Henry peered down at the GPS. "It looks like this one is about a quarter mile straight ahead."

The Aldens followed the trail up and down

a hill, over a small wooden bridge, and into a thicker part of the woods.

"It should be right around here now," Henry said.

The children split up and checked various trees. While they were searching, a boy and a girl came charging down the trail. They wore matching denim jackets and looked a lot alike. They were the same height, same weight, and they had the same shade of brown hair. The girl wore hers in a long braid down her back. They looked around Jessie's age.

The boy held something in his hand that looked a lot like a GPS. Were they geocachers, too? Henry wondered.

"This way!" The boy stared at the gadget in his hand. The two veered off the path and headed straight for Benny.

"Hello," Benny said to them.

They ignored Benny, their eyes fixed on the gadget in the boy's hand. Then the girl walked around behind Benny. She bent down and pulled a metal container out of the hollow in the bottom of the tree.

"Oh, you found it," Benny said.

"Looks like we were looking for the same thing," Henry said cheerfully as he, Jessie, and Violet joined them.

"We're the Aldens," Jessie said. "I'm Jessie. This is Henry, Violet, and Benny."

"That's nice," the boy said absently. He and the girl knelt down on the ground pried the lid off the container together.

"Is it in there?" the girl asked once the lid was off.

"Yes!" the boy exclaimed. He pulled out a stuffed armadillo and the girl squealed in delight as she took it from him.

"Hey, that looks a lot like the armadillo we found in another cache yesterday," Violet said.

The girl looked up at Violet. "Was it the 'Walk in the Park' cache?"

"Yes, I think so," Violet said.

The girl rolled her eyes. "Then of course it's the same armadillo. It's a travel bug!"

"What's a travel bug?" Jessie asked.

But the mysterious boy and girl didn't

answer. They stood up and the girl put the armadillo in her pocket.

"We got what we came for," the girl told the Aldens. "You guys can put the cache back."

Then they left as quickly as they'd arrived.

"That was odd," Jessie said.

"They sure weren't very friendly," Henry said.

"They didn't even put anything in the box when they took the armadillo," Benny said.

"I wonder why they wanted the armadillo so badly," Violet said.

"They said it was a travel bug," Jessie said. "What's a travel bug?"

"I don't know," Henry said. "But I think I know where we can find out."

CHAPTER 4

The Club Meeting

On Friday morning, Grandfather drove the children to the nature center so they could go to the Greenfield Geocachers club meeting. When Grandfather dropped them off, they saw a crowd of people milling around the patio and picnic area in front of the nature center. There were families, college students, and retired couples. Many of the people had dogs with them.

"We should've brought Watch," Benny said.

"Maybe next time," Henry said.

"Hey, Boxcar Kids!" Andy Robertson waved at the Aldens.

"Hi, Andy," Jessie said as the Aldens made their way over to him. The Aldens were glad to see someone they knew.

"I'm glad you came to the meeting," Andy said. "We're just waiting for Cal Edwards to come and unlock the nature center for us. Then we'll get started."

"Cal Edwards is in this club?" Violet asked.

"He sure is," Andy replied. "In fact, he's our club secretary. Why? Do you know him?"

"Yes," Jessie said. "He's a friend of our grandfather's."

"That's wonderful," Andy said. "Cal was one of the people who started this club."

"How did geocaching start?" Violet wanted to know.

"It's a neat story," Andy said. "One person started the whole thing. He was a computer consultant and he wanted to see how well his GPS worked. So he hid a container out in the woods. Then he posted the coordinates online. Sure enough, someone else was able to find the container using a GPS! From there, the idea grew."

"And now people all over the world do this?" Jessie asked. "Wow!"

"Let me introduce you to some of the club members while we wait," Andy offered.

He turned to the brown-haired man and woman who were seated at the picnic table behind him. "This is Mr. and Mrs. Zeller," Andy said. "And these are the Aldens: Henry, Jessie, Violet, and Benny. The Aldens are new to geocaching, but they want to join our group."

"That's good," Mrs. Zeller said, smiling at the children.

"You know, we have a boy and a girl about your age," Mr. Zeller said. "Zack and Zoe. They're twins." He glanced around. "I'm not sure where they are right now."

"They're probably giving our son a hard time," said a tall man who came up behind them. He had dark hair and dark eyes.

His wife stood a head shorter, but she also had dark hair and dark eyes. Neither one of them smiled.

The Zellers exchanged looks. They did not look happy to see this other couple.

"Perhaps *your* son is giving Zack and Zoe a hard time," Mrs. Zeller said stiffly.

Andy stepped in between the adults. "Mr. and Mrs. Greene, have you met the Aldens?"

The tall man nodded at the children.

"Nice to meet you," his wife said coolly.

"The Greenes have a son around your age, Jessie," Andy said. "His name is David."

"Oh, maybe we can meet him?" Jessie said.

"I'm not sure where he is right now," Mr. Greene said.

"Let's see if we can find him," Mrs. Greene said. Then they walked away.

"We should find out where Zack and Zoe went, too," Mrs. Zeller said, getting up from the picnic table.

"It was nice meeting you all," Mr. Zeller

said. Then he and his wife went off in the opposite direction from the Greenes.

"Those people don't seem to like each other very much," Benny said.

"There's a little rivalry between those two families," Andy said as he checked his watch.

"What kind of rivalry?" Jessie asked.

"Well, right now our club has a contest going on. Whoever finds the most caches this month wins a new GPS."

"Wow!" Violet said. "That's a good prize."

"Yes, it is," Andy said. "The Zellers and the Greenes do a lot of geocaching. Probably more than anyone else in the club. And I know they both want to win that prize."

"Well, there are only a few days left in the month, so I don't think we'll win the prize," Henry said. "But we did do a little more geocaching the other day."

"You did?" Andy smiled. "Did you find any caches."

"Well, we couldn't find the first two we

looked for," Jessie said. "But we found the third one. It was called 'Chipmunk Challenge.'"

"Actually, another boy and girl found it before we did," Violet said. "There was a stuffed armadillo inside. It looked just like the one we found in the Walk in the Park cache with you."

"In fact, the kids who found it said it was the *same* armadillo," Jessie added. "They said it was a travel bug, but we never found out what that meant. What is a travel bug, Andy?"

"A travel bug is something that travels from one cache to another," Andy explained. "Sometimes a travel bug has a goal. For instance, maybe it's trying to visit caches in all fifty states, or maybe it's trying to visit cities that start with a certain letter. If you can help it reach its goal, you can take it. Otherwise you should leave it for someone else to take."

"How can you tell whether something is a travel bug or not?" Henry asked.

"If it's a travel bug, it should have a tag

attached to it that tells you it's a travel bug. There will be a tracking number on the tag. You can use that number to get to the travel bug's own page on the geocaching website and see where the travel bug has been."

"Cool!" Benny said.

All of a sudden the Aldens heard raised voices behind them. They turned and saw the brown-haired boy and girl in matching denim jackets arguing with a dark-haired boy wearing a green baseball cap.

"Tell us!" the girl demanded as she flipped her braid over her shoulder. "Tell us how many caches you guys have found this month."

The boy in the baseball cap shook his head. "I'm not going to tell you," he said with a grin. "But it's probably more than you've found!"

"It is not," the other boy argued. "Otherwise you'd tell us how many you've found."

The Aldens looked at each other. "Isn't that the same boy and girl we ran into out when we were looking for the Chipmunk Challenge cache?" Jessie asked.

"I think so," Violet said.

"That's Zack and Zoe Zeller," Andy said. "The other boy is David Greene."

Mr. and Mrs. Zeller led their children to one side of the crowd and Mr. and Mrs. Greene led their son to the other side.

"Hey, are we going to start this meeting or not?" Mr. Greene called out.

"I wonder where Cal is," an older man said, checking his watch. "Our meeting was supposed to start ten minutes ago."

"I don't think Cal has ever missed a meeting," Andy's dad, Mr. Robertson, said.

"There was one time he missed one," Mrs. Zeller said. "He was out of town. But he gave someone else a key to the nature center so we could get in."

"We could try calling him," Andy said.

"I'll try," Mr. Zeller said. He pulled a cell phone out of his pocket. "I think I've even got his cell phone number right here."

Mr. Zeller dialed, then put his phone to his ear.

Everyone waited.

After a couple of seconds, Mr. Zeller said, "He must have his phone turned off. It didn't even ring once."

"He's probably on his way," Mr. Robertson said. "Maybe we should just go ahead and start without him? It's a nice day. I don't mind holding our meeting out here. Do any of you?"

No one did. So they all made themselves comfortable on picnic tables, benches and the grass. Then, as president of the club, Andy's dad called the meeting to order.

Everyone went around and introduced themselves, and Andy introduced the Aldens.

Then Mr. Robertson asked, "Is there any new business to discuss?"

"Yes." Mr. Zeller raised his hand. "There are a few caches in the area that seem to be missing."

Jessie and Henry looked at one another. Were these the same caches that they couldn't find?

Mr. Greene chuckled. "Are you sure they're missing? Maybe you and your family just couldn't find them."

Mr. Zeller frowned. "Of course I'm sure."

"We always find the cache when we're out geocaching!" Zack called out.

"I don't know," David teased. "I can remember one that you guys had a little trouble with last summer."

"That's because the river was high and we couldn't get to it," Zoe said hotly. "We knew where to look."

"I'm telling you, some of these caches are missing," Mr. Zeller said. "And I think they've been stolen!"

"Stolen?" Several people gasped.

"You know, we were out looking for the Squires Point cache the other day and we couldn't find it," a woman in a blue scarf said.

"Hey, that's one of the ones we were looking for," Benny spoke up. "We couldn't find it, either."

"I don't know about that one," Mr. Zeller said. "But I know for a fact the Happy Hollow cache has been stolen."

"How do you 'know for a fact?'" Mr.

Greene asked with a smirk.

Mr. Zeller looked irritated. "Because we've been to that one before," he replied. "There was supposed to be a travel bug in there, so we thought we'd pick it up and take it to another cache. But when we arrived at the spot, the cache wasn't there."

"When did you look for it?" a young college student asked. "My roommate and I looked for it a week ago. It was right where it was supposed to be."

"This was just a couple days ago," Mr. Zeller said. He turned to the Aldens. "When did you kids go looking for it?"

"Two days ago," Henry replied. "We couldn't find Muffy's Hideaway, either. But we're brand new geocachers. Maybe we just couldn't find them."

"I don't know," an older man in overalls said. "My wife and I were out looking for that Muffy's Hideaway yesterday and we couldn't find it, either."

"I hate to say it, but I think Mr. Zeller is right," said the woman in the blue scarf. "I think we have a thief on our hands."

"Wait a minute," Henry said. "Isn't it possible that someone who doesn't know about geocaching took a couple of caches?" After all, the Aldens had almost walked away with a cache themselves, not knowing what it was.

"I'd believe that if it was just one cache that was missing," the man in overalls said. "But there are several missing. I think someone is taking them on purpose."

"Do we know how many caches are missing for sure?" Mr. Robertson asked. "Or which ones are missing?"

No one did.

"I've got a list of all the caches hidden around Greenfield," Mr. Greene said, holding up a brown folder. "Maybe we should look for them all at once and find out which ones are missing."

"That's a great idea," Mr. Robertson said. "Let's divide up the list so that everyone here gets to look for two or three caches."

"If we can search over the weekend, maybe we can all meet again on Monday to report what we've found," Mr. Zeller said.

As everyone got up to leave, Mr. Robertson glanced over at the Aldens. "Are you kids interested in helping out?"

"Sure," Henry said.

"Why don't you see if you can find these two." Mr. Robertson tore off a sheet of paper and handed it to Henry.

The children looked at the paper. Their assignment was to find the 'Nesting Place' cache and the 'Round the World' cache.

"We'll look for these this afternoon," Jessie promised.

"Do you think there really is a thief stealing all the caches?" Benny asked his brother and sisters as they headed home.

"I don't know," Henry said. "It's possible that some of us just haven't been able to find some of the caches."

"But there are quite a few people who looked for some of the same caches," Jessie said. "It's strange none of us could find them."

"And Mr. Zeller said his family had been

to the Happy Hollow cache before," Violet added. "So they knew where to look for it, but they still couldn't find it. That makes me wonder if someone is stealing the caches."

"But who would do such a thing?" Benny asked. "And why?"

Jessie shrugged. "It's a mystery."

CHAPTER 5

The Search Is On!

"Let me get this straight," Grandfather said after Henry explained what they wanted. "You want me to give you a ride to the new mall, but you're not sure you're actually *going* to the mall?"

Violet giggled. "That's right."

"We're looking for more geocaches," said Jessie. "That's why we don't know exactly where we want to go."

"Ah." Grandfather nodded knowingly. "More geocaching. Sure, I'll give you a ride.

I have some errands to run out that way, anyway."

"Thank you, Grandfather," the children said.

"Should we bring Watch?" Benny asked as he scratched his dog's ears.

Everyone else turned to look at Watch, who wagged his tail when he heard his name.

"Of course we should bring him," Violet said. "He's our geo-dog! A lot of people at the geocaching club had dogs."

"Okay, Watch," Henry said, clapping his hands. "Let's go find your leash."

Watch barked once, then ran for the back porch, where they kept his leash.

Henry snapped the leash to Watch's collar, then they all got in the car.

Violet and Benny sat in the back seat and watched the GPS as Grandfather drove toward the new mall. They had the GPS set to find the 'Nesting Place' cache first.

Benny announced when they were 5 miles from the cache. Then 3 miles. Then 2 miles. Then 1 mile. When Grandfather pulled into the mall parking lot, the GPS still said they were half a mile from the cache.

"That's okay," Henry said. "Half a mile isn't far to walk."

Grandfather pulled up in front of a small coffee shop across the street from the mall. "I'll go run my errands, then I'll come back here and read the paper," Grandfather said. "I'll meet you in the coffee shop in an hour and a half."

The children agreed. Then they got out of the car. Henry held Watch's leash and Benny held the GPS.

"So, which way, Benny?" Jessie asked after their grandfather had driven off.

"That way," Benny said, pointing to the shopping center.

Henry saw how close they were to the building, then glanced down at the GPS in Benny's hand. "I wonder if it's behind the mall," Henry said.

"Maybe," Violet said. "Let's walk around and see."

There was a small parking lot behind the

mall and a wide grassy area behind that. The grass went all the way to the woods. A row of bluebird houses sat at the edge of the woods.

"Ah, now we know where the 'Nesting Place' cache got its name," Jessie said.

Something in the woods caught Watch's attention. He started barking and pulling on his leash. The Aldens looked toward the woods and spotted four people dressed in matching blue jackets: a mom, dad, and two kids. They stopped at the edge of the woods and stared back at the Aldens.

"Hey, isn't that the Zellers?" Benny asked.

Violet squinted. "It's hard to tell for sure from way back here, but it does kind of look like them," she said.

"Hey, Mr. and Mrs. Zeller!" Benny called, waving his arms. "Is that you?"

The people, whoever they were, immediately turned around and disappeared into the woods.

"That was strange," Henry said.

"Maybe it wasn't the Zellers after all,"

Jessie said with a shrug. "How far are we from the cache, Benny?"

"Not far," Benny replied. "About 80 feet."

The Aldens followed the GPS until the arrow started spinning. Then they started looking around.

They were right between two bluebird houses. There were no trees or bushes for a cache to be hiding in.

"Do you think it's inside one of these houses?" Jessie asked.

"I wouldn't think so," Henry said. "I don't think the birds would like that very much."

Benny walked all around one of the birdhouses. He jumped up to see the top, then peered underneath. "Hey, there's something stuck under here."

Henry, Jessie, and Violet bent down and looked under the birdhouse. A small black box about the size of a deck of cards was stuck to the bottom of the birdhouse.

"I don't think that's it, Benny," Jessie said. "It's not big enough."

But Benny pulled the box off the bird house

anyway. "Hey, it's magnetic. There's a piece of metal screwed into the bottom of the birdhouse and that's how the box was stuck to it."

Benny opened up the box. The inside lid read, *Official Micro Cache. Congratulations! You've found it!* The box held a folded paper that was half-filled with nicknames of geocachers and a tiny pencil.

"I think this is it," Benny said. He held the box so everyone could see it.

"I think you're right, Benny," Violet said. "I read about micro caches on the geocaching website. They're really tiny caches. You usually don't trade anything in a micro cache. You just write that you found it."

"Well, at least this one isn't missing," Henry said.

"It looks like this piece of paper is the log," Jessie said as she took it out of the box and unfolded it. "Most people just signed their nickname and their date. Do you want to sign it, Benny? Then we can see if we can find the other cache."

"Okay," Benny said. He took the paper back from Jessie and laid it flat against the birdhouse. Using the birdhouse as a table, he wrote "Boxcar Kids" and the date in his best handwriting on the next line.

Then Jessie took the GPS and set it to the Round the World cache. "It looks like the other cache is three-quarters of a mile southwest of here," she said.

Benny folded the piece of paper, stuffed it back in the box, and closed it up. Then he put the box back where he found it underneath the birdhouse.

"Let's go," Henry said. He gave a little tug on the leash and Watch turned around and headed back across the parking lot with the children.

They walked around to the other side of the mall, then followed the GPS straight west.

"Hey, look!" Violet pointed straight ahead. "There's a little playground over there past those houses." The playground sat on a triangle of land where three streets came together. It was just big enough for a tetherball, slide, and a row of swings.

"I didn't know that playground was there. Did you guys?" Jessie asked.

"No," Henry replied. "That's one of the fun things about geocaching. It takes you places you might not have gone to otherwise."

Benny leaned over and checked the GPS in Jessie's hand. "Well, the GPS is pointing straight ahead," he said. "And we're getting close. Just a little over 200 feet to go. So I bet the cache is in the playground."

"Isn't 'round the world' a game you can play with tetherball?" Violet asked.

"I think so," Henry said. "Maybe the cache is around the tetherball."

They crossed the street and spread out around the tetherball post. There was a tree with a hollowed-out spot behind the tetherball area. Benny ran to the hollow, but there was nothing inside.

Jessie and Violet checked the swings. Henry and Watch checked under the slide. But nobody found anything.

"Where could it be?" Violet asked, turning around.

They checked the flower bed and all the stones around the flower bed. They checked bushes. Then they checked all the playground equipment again, just in case they'd missed something the first time. But they didn't find the cache.

"I think this one is missing," Henry said.

"Let's check the whole playground one more time," Jessie said. "I'd hate to think we just didn't look in the right place."

So the children combed the playground one more time. But they still didn't find anything.

"I give up," Violet said, plopping down on the grass. "The Round the World cache is definitely missing."

"Do you think someone stole it?" Benny asked.

"I don't know," Jessie said. But she was wondering the same thing. Maybe there really was a thief who was trying to ruin the geocachers' fun?

CHAPTER 6

Who's the Thief?

There were a lot of people standing around outside the nature center on Monday when the Aldens arrived. Once again the door was locked.

"Doggie!" a little girl squealed as the Aldens joined the group. Jessie held Watch on a leash. There were several other dogs in the crowd, too.

The Aldens stopped and let the little girl pet Watch.

Just behind them, the Zeller twins were

arguing with David Greene.

"We are way better at geocaching than you guys," Zack claimed.

"Oh, sure you are," David replied. "That's why you guys couldn't find one of the caches you were supposed to find over the weekend."

"We couldn't find it because someone stole it!" Zoe cried, hands on her hips.

"I think you just couldn't find it because you're not good geocachers," David said.

The little girl had finished petting Watch, so the Aldens moved away from the Greenes and the Zellers. All that arguing made the Aldens uncomfortable.

"Remember what Andy told us? There's a rivalry between those two families," Henry said.

"That may be," Jessie said, stopping to let Watch nuzzle noses with a beagle. "But sometimes their arguing sounds a little mean."

The Aldens found Andy Robertson and his dad up by the door to the nature center. Mr. Robertson was talking to an older man with a red baseball cap. They all looked worried.

"What's the matter?" Jessie asked.

"We're just wondering where Cal could be," Mr. Robertson said, scratching his chin. "Nobody here has heard from him in nearly a week."

"We saw him at the dog park that day we met you last week," Henry said. "But we haven't seen him since."

"Several people here have called him and left messages, but he hasn't returned any of the calls," Andy said.

The older man in the baseball cap nodded. "I've been volunteering here for six years and I've never arrived to find the doors locked. I don't think Cal's ever missed a day of work in his life. As far as I know, he's the only one who has a key. He certainly wouldn't close the nature center without telling the volunteers."

"What if something bad happened?" Benny asked. "Maybe he was out hiking without his GPS and got lost in the woods. Maybe a mountain lion got him!"

"I don't think there are any mountain lions around here, son," the man in the baseball cap said, patting Benny on the back. "Wherever Cal is, I'm sure there's a logical explanation for why he hasn't called. I just wish we knew what it was."

"Well, maybe we should go ahead and hold our meeting outside again," Mr. Robertson said. He walked toward the crowd and whistled to get everyone's attention.

The club members talked a little more about Cal and how strange it was that he would just disappear without telling anyone where he was. Then the talk turned to the missing caches.

"The other mystery," Benny whispered.

"What do you mean?" Violet whispered back.

"There are two mysteries here: where is Cal is one mystery, and what happened to the missing caches is the other mystery," Benny said.

"Did you all have a chance to go check the geocaches you were assigned to over the weekend?" Mr. Robertson asked.

Everyone nodded.

"I've got my list of caches right here," Mr. Greene said, opening his clipboard. "Let's just go down the list and see which ones were found and which ones weren't."

Jessie opened her backpack and pulled out a small notebook and pencil. "I think I'll make a list of which ones are missing, too," she told Henry, Violet, and Benny.

It took about ten minutes to go through the entire list. When Mr. Greene finished, Jessie had a list of eight caches that were missing.

"That's a lot of missing caches," a man in a gray sweatshirt said.

"I wouldn't be surprised if we missed one or two," the woman next to him said. "But I don't think we would miss eight of them."

Several other people nodded.

"That proves there's a thief in Greenfield," Mr. Zeller declared.

"But why would someone steal our caches?" one of the college students asked. "There isn't anything valuable in them."

"Someone just wants to ruin our fun," the man in the gray sweatshirt said.

"Do you think more caches are going to go missing?" Andy asked with concern.

"Could be," Mr. Zeller said.

"What are we going to do about the contest if all our caches start disappearing?" the man in the gray sweatshirt asked.

"Maybe we'll have to cancel the contest this month," Mr. Greene said.

"We shouldn't cancel it," Zoe Zeller said, tossing her brown braid over her shoulder.

"Yeah," her brother, Zack, added. "We can just say that whoever's found the most caches so far wins! I'm sure that's us." Zack smiled.

"Now, wait a minute—" David Greene interrupted.

Mr. Robertson raised his hands for order. "I don't think we have to give up on the contest just yet. Let's see what happens. Let's see if the missing caches turn up. Let's see if other caches go missing."

"Good idea," several people agreed.

The meeting broke up shortly after that. The Aldens stayed and talked with Andy for a few minutes, then they decided to walk home through the woods so they could stop at the dog park and let Watch run around.

"I sure hope we can figure out what happened to all those missing caches," Violet said as she kicked at an acorn on the path.

"I hope that more caches don't go missing," Benny said, holding tight to Watch's leash.

"Me, too," Jessie said.

All of a sudden Violet grabbed Jessie's arm. "Shh!" she hissed. "I hear something."

Everyone stopped and listened. Watch sat down on the path and cocked his head. At first all they heard was the wind through the trees. Then they heard voices.

The Aldens crept closer and peered around a big tree. They saw the Zeller twins sitting on a log talking.

"Maybe we should put them back," Zack said.

"No, not yet," Zoe said.

Watch barked and the twins looked up. They scowled at the Aldens. "Why are you guys always following us around?" Zack asked.

"Are you spying on us?" Zoe asked.

But before the Aldens could answer, the twins took off toward the nature center.

"That was strange," Violet said.

"And what did Zack mean when he said, 'maybe we should put them back?'" Jessie wondered. "Put *what* back?"

"The caches?" Benny asked. "Did they take the missing caches?"

"Why would they do that?" Violet asked.

"They're members of the geocaching club. They don't want the caches to go missing any more than anyone else in the club does."

"Except they're trying to win the prize for most caches found," Jessie said. "If some of the caches go missing, then other people— like the Greenes—won't find them."

"And then maybe the Zellers will win the contest," Benny said.

"I don't know," Henry said. "We shouldn't

jump to conclusions. Zoe and Zack could've been talking about anything."

"Yeah, but I still think we should keep an eye on them," Benny said.

"I agree," Jessie said.

* * * *

The next morning, the telephone rang bright and early at the Alden house. The children weren't even out of bed yet.

Violet rolled over and looked at the clock on the nightstand between her bed and Jessie's. "It's only 7:30," Violet said with a yawn as the telephone rang again. "Who could be calling us so early?"

"I don't know," Jessie replied. She threw her covers off and stumbled to the telephone in the upstairs hallway. Violet was right behind her.

"Hello?" Jessie said in a raspy voice.

"Jessie? This is Andy. I'm sorry to call so early. Did I wake you?"

The boys' bedroom door opened then

and Henry and Benny stepped out into the hallway.

"It's okay, Andy," Jessie said. "I was just getting up anyway. What's up?" Violet, Henry, and Benny squeezed in so they could hear, too.

"My dad and I were out geocaching this morning," Andy began. "We were going to grab the travel bug out of the 'Strike Three' cache because we're going to visit my grandma in Pine City tomorrow. So we thought we'd put the travel bug at a cache near my grandma's house. Except now we can't."

"Oh, no," Jessie said. "Is the travel bug missing?"

"The whole cache is missing," Andy said.

"That's terrible," Jessie said.

"We found something else in its place, though," Andy said. "A folded up piece of paper."

"Did you open it?" Jessie asked. "Was there anything written on the paper?"

"Just two words," Andy said. "'Ha-ha.'"

CHAPTER 7

Late Night Clues

"'Ha-ha'," Benny read the two words on the paper on the table in front of him. The words were written in red crayon and they took up most of the page. "What does that mean?"

"That's what we'd all like to know," Andy said, his hands wrapped around a steaming mug of hot cocoa.

After talking on the phone, Andy and the Aldens decided to meet at the coffee shop to discuss the mysterious note Andy and his dad had found.

"It sounds like someone is laughing at us," Violet said glumly.

Jessie took a sip of her cocoa, then said, "I don't think they're laughing at *us* exactly. I think they're laughing at whoever found the paper."

"Yeah, it's like a joke on them because they were expecting to find a geocache and instead they found this note," Benny said.

"Then whoever left this note is probably our thief," Henry said, leaning back against his chair.

"That's right," Andy agreed. He broke off a piece of his pastry and nibbled on it.

"So, who left the note?" Violet asked.

No one had any ideas.

"Could it be someone who knows what geocaching is, but they're not a member of the geocaching club?" Jessie asked.

"Why would they steal the caches?" Henry asked. "What would they get out of it?"

"I don't know," Jessie said. "Maybe they just don't like the geocaching club for some reason?"

"How can the geocaching club be bothering anyone?" Violet asked. "It's not a private club. Anyone who wants to can join."

"And all the caches are hidden on public property," Andy pointed out. "So it can't be someone who doesn't like people trespassing on their property."

Andy and the Aldens were stumped.

Jessie finished the last of her cocoa, then set her mug down. "Was the Strike Three cache there last weekend when we all went out and checked on all the caches around Greenfield?" she asked.

"Yes," Andy replied. "The Zellers were assigned to that one. They said it was there over the weekend."

"The Zellers were the last people to find this cache?" Benny asked.

"I think so," Andy said. "Their nickname is the Zees. I'm pretty sure theirs was the last entry in the online log."

"What about the Greenes?" Benny asked. "Have they found this cache before?"

"I don't know," Andy replied. "Their nickname

is the Green Lights. I didn't notice if they'd signed the online log. Why?"

Benny shrugged. "Maybe the Zellers would have taken that cache to play a trick on the Greenes."

"Yeah, maybe they did it so the Greenes wouldn't find it and then they'd be ahead in the contest," Violet said. "They really want to win that contest at the end of the month."

"So do the Greenes," Jessie pointed out.

"But do you really think either family wants to win badly enough that they'd steal some of the caches?" Henry asked.

"I don't know," Andy said. "My dad said the geocaching club might have to break up if these caches keep disappearing."

"Oh, no!" Violet said.

"That would be terrible," Benny said.

"I don't think either the Zellers or the Greenes want to see the club end," Henry said.

"Nobody does," Andy said. "But there's no point in having a club if all our caches are going to disappear."

"Well, what can we do to make sure more caches don't disappear?" Violet asked.

"I don't know," Andy said with a shrug. "That's the problem. We can't very well stake them all out and try to catch the thief in the act. There are too many caches to watch."

"And too many hours in a day," Henry said.

"So all we can do is wait for the thief to strike again?" Jessie asked.

"Or try to figure out where he or she might strike next and be ready," Violet said. "Which is almost impossible!"

Andy nodded. "Do you see why my dad is so frustrated?"

"If only Cal was here," Jessie said. "Maybe he'd have some ideas."

* * * *

"What are you doing, Jessie?" Violet asked. It was nine o'clock and the girls were ready for bed.

Violet had come downstairs for a drink of water and found Jessie sitting at the computer. Jessie was staring at the geocaching website.

Her notebook lay open on the desk in front of her.

"I'm just looking at the information for all these missing caches to see what they have in common," Jessie said.

"Have you found anything yet?" Henry asked as he and Benny walked into the family room. They were dressed in their pajamas, too.

"Nope," Jessie said, resting her chin in her hands. "They're all different kinds of caches. They're all located in different parts of town. Some are rated easy to find; others are rated hard. It seems like the only thing they have in common is that they're all missing."

"Did you ever look to see whether the Greenes visited the Strike Three cache?" Benny asked.

"No, I didn't," Jessie said. "But we can look right now."

The children pulled up chairs while Jessie pulled up the website for the Strike Three cache. She scrolled through the log.

"Here it is," Jessie said, pointing to an

entry signed by the Green Lights. "It looks like they were here three days before the Zellers were."

"Then I don't think the Zellers would have taken that cache," Henry said. "What would be the point? They've already counted that cache for the contest. And so have the Greenes."

"And the Greenes wouldn't have any reason to come back and steal it after the Zellers already found it, either," Jessie said.

"I wonder if the Greenes and the Zellers have both found all the other missing caches," Violet said.

"Let's check," Jessie said, reaching for the mouse.

While Jessie scrolled through the information on each of the missing caches, Henry took notes.

When they finished going through all eight, Henry looked at the paper in front of him. "It looks like both the Greenes and the Zellers have visited all of them," he said.

"If both families have already been to all

those missing caches before they disappeared, neither one is gaining anything by taking them and preventing the other family from finding them. They've already found them!" Jessie said.

Violet and Benny nodded. But Henry just stared at the computer screen. All of a sudden he sat up a little straighter.

"Can we scroll back through the other missing caches one more time?" Henry asked.

Jessie turned to him. "Did you see something?"

"Maybe," Henry said. "I don't need to read all the logs. I just need to see the main page for each one."

"What are you looking for?" Benny yawned. He wasn't used to being up so late.

Henry pointed to the screen. "Look at this line," he said.

"It says, 'placed by Hammer Ed,'" Violet read. "So?"

"Look at who placed all the other caches," Henry said.

The children all leaned closer to the screen and watched as Jessie loaded the information for each of the missing caches.

"They were all placed by Hammer Ed," Violet said.

Benny yawned again. "So who's Hammer Ed?"

"That's a good question," Henry said.

CHAPTER 8

Where Is Cal?

"I have a surprise for you," Mrs. Mac-Gregor announced when the children sat down to breakfast the next morning.

"What?" Benny asked eagerly.

"It smells like . . . scrambled eggs," Violet said, breathing in the delicious smell.

"But it doesn't look like scrambled eggs," Jessie said as Mrs. MacGregor set a plate of stuffed burritos in the middle of the table. "It looks like breakfast burritos."

"Yum!" Benny said. "What's inside them?"

"You'll have to bite into them to find out," Mrs. MacGregor said with a smile.

"Hooray! Geocaches we can eat!" Benny said, reaching for a burrito.

Everyone laughed.

"And just think, we didn't have to use a GPS to find them," Henry said.

"No. All we needed was our noses!" Violet said. "Our noses led us straight to the kitchen."

"It looks like there are eggs, sausage, onions, peppers, tomatoes, and cheese in the burritos," Jessie said. "These are very good, Mrs. MacGregor."

"Thank you, Jessie," Mrs. MacGregor said. "I'm glad you like them."

While the children ate, the talk turned to Hammer Ed, the person who had first placed all the missing caches. Who could Hammer Ed be, they wondered.

"Have we met anyone at the geocaching club named Ed?" Jessie asked as she dished up some fruit for herself, then passed the bowl to Henry.

"Not that I remember," Henry replied.

Benny helped himself to another burrito. "Have we met someone who likes to build stuff?" he asked.

"Maybe we have," Violet said. "But we don't know it. All we really know about any of the people in the club is that they like geocaching."

"It's too bad Andy and his dad are visiting Andy's grandma," Henry said. "Otherwise we could call and ask them. They probably know everyone in the club."

"They might even know who uses the nickname Hammer Ed," Jessie said. "Andy knew the Zellers' nickname and the Greenes' nickname."

"You know who else would probably know all the club members?" Violet said. "Cal would. Andy said he was one of the people who started the geocaching club."

"Yeah, but nobody knows where Cal is," Benny said.

"People have tried calling him, but I wonder if anyone has actually gone to his house to see if he's home," Jessie said as she wiped her mouth with her napkin.

"I wonder," Henry said.

"If he's not home, maybe we can figure out where he went," Violet said.

Henry nodded. "If everyone's done eating, we can go right now," he said, pushing back his chair.

"Wait! Can I have one more burrito before we go?" Benny asked.

Violet laughed. "You've already had three!"

"I know," Benny said. "But they're geo-caching burritos! Maybe if I eat another one, it will help us solve this mystery!"

While Benny gobbled up another burrito, the other children looked up Cal's address in the phone book. He lived on Seventeenth Street.

Then, when Benny finally said he was full, the children set off on their bikes for Cal's house.

It was a warm but windy day, and the children found themselves pedaling against the wind for much of the ride. Empty garbage cans and recycling bins that had been left outside were rolling all around the road.

"Looks like it's garbage day in this neighborhood," Violet said as she swerved around a green garbage can.

"Looks like it," Jessie agreed.

The Aldens turned onto Seventeeth Street and started pedaling uphill.

"What's the house number again?" Benny asked.

"It's 214," Henry replied.

They rode past 126, 130, and 134 Seventeenth Street.

"It should be in the next block," Jessie puffed. She was pedaling so hard she was starting to sweat. "And it'll be on the right side of the street."

"I see 206, 210, 214! There it is!" Benny cried. "The little white house up on the hill."

The Aldens rode into the driveway and parked their bikes in front of the garage.

"Cal's garbage can isn't outside," Jessie noted.

"Unless it's one of those that blew all the

way down the street," Benny said as he put his kickstand down.

There was a fenced patio on top of the garage and two sets of steps leading to the front porch. When the Aldens reached the top, they counted three folded newspapers lying on the mat in front of the door. Jessie lifted the lid on the small black mailbox. It was almost full of envelopes and flyers.

"Well, I think we know why there's no garbage can in front of Cal's house," Jessie said. "He's obviously not home."

They were about to turn around and start back down the stairs when they heard a dog barking. The barking was coming from inside the house.

The Aldens glanced at each other in surprise.

"That sounds like Chester," Benny said.

"Why would Cal go away and leave Chester home alone?" Jessie asked.

"I don't know," Henry replied. "I don't think he would do that. But if there was somebody staying here and taking care of Chester, wouldn't they bring the newspapers and mail inside?"

Benny rang the doorbell and the children waited anxiously for someone to come to the door. But no one did.

The children walked down the first set of steps and over to the fence where they could see into the patio. There was a large picnic table in the middle. A hammer, a roll of duct tape, and an open jar of nails lay loose on the picnic table.

"That's odd," Henry said. "Why would Cal leave all this stuff sitting outside?"

"I don't know," Jessie said. "It looks like he was about to fix something."

"What was he about to fix?" Violet asked.

Nobody knew.

"Hey!" a voice called from behind them. The Aldens turned and saw an older, heavy-set woman standing in the yard next door. She did not look happy.

"What do you kids think you're doing?"

"We're looking for Cal Edwards," Henry said, walking over to the edge of the yard. "Have you seen him in the last few days?"

"May I ask your names?" the woman asked.

"Sure," Jessie replied. "We're the Aldens. I'm Jessie, and this is my sister, Violet, and my brothers, Henry and Benny."

The woman's face softened. "I'm Mrs. Michaelson," she said. "Mr. Edwards is out of town."

"He is?" Henry said with surprise. "But his dog, Chester, is here."

"Yes, I know," Mrs. Michaelson said. "His mother broke her hip and she needed help right away. So I've been taking care of Chester. I've been feeding him and letting him out. I'd let him stay with me, but I have four cats and I don't think he'd be very happy at my house."

"Oh," Violet said with relief. She was sorry to hear about Cal's mother, but she was glad he was okay, and she was glad he hadn't left Chester completely alone.

"We didn't know," Jessie said. "We saw all the newspapers and mail—"

"Yes, I imagine the mailbox is getting

pretty full. I don't pick up the mail or newspapers every day because it's so hard for me to go up all those steps. I've been going in through the garage to take care of Chester. His things are all in the basement, so then I don't have to go up any steps."

"Oh, we can bring the mail and newspapers to you," Violet offered.

"Would you?" Mrs. Michaelson looked thankful. "That would be a big help."

"Sure," Benny said. "Come on, Violet. Let's go!"

While Benny and Violet ran back up the steps, Jessie and Henry talked to Mrs. Michaelson some more.

"How long has Cal been gone?" Henry asked.

"He left last Monday as soon as he got the call," Mrs. Michaelson replied. "But he phoned yesterday to say his mother is getting better and he'll be coming back soon."

"That's good," Jessie said.

Benny and Violet returned with Cal's newspapers and mail and handed them all to Mrs Michaelson.

"Thank you, children," she said.

"You're welcome," Benny said.

"I'm so glad Cal and Chester are okay," Violet said.

The children said good-bye to Mrs. Michaelson, then headed back to their bikes.

"Well, there's one mystery solved," Benny said as he swung his leg over the back of his bike. "We know what happened to Cal. Now all we have to do is figure out who Hammer Ed is and what happened to all those missing caches."

"Wait a minute," Violet said, holding onto her bike. "Do you remember what Mrs. Michaelson called Cal?"

"Sure," Jessie said. "She called him Mr. Edwards. That's his name."

Violet grinned. "That's right. His name is Mr. *Ed*wards."

"Oh!" Benny said, grinning back at Violet. "And Mr. *Ed*wards likes to fix stuff."

"So maybe Cal Edwards is Hammer Ed?"

Jessie asked.

"I'll bet he is!" Henry said.

"Then I guess we've solved two mysteries," Benny said. "We know what happened to Cal and we know who Hammer Ed is."

"But we still don't know what happened to the missing caches," Henry said.

"We'll figure it out," Jessie said.

"We'd better," Benny said.

CHAPTER 9

Benny's Theory

The Aldens followed the bike path through North Ridge Park on their way home from Cal's house. The trees sheltered them from the wind, so it was easier pedaling here.

The bike path became a narrow dirt trail through the thickest part of the woods and the children had to ride single file. As they rode down one hill, they heard voices coming from the top of the next hill. Angry voices.

"Let go!" a boy's voice said.

"No, you let go!" a girl answered.

"You're not supposed to take them!"

"We're not taking them, we're protecting them!"

When the Aldens reached the top of the hill, they saw the Zeller twins and David Greene over by a huge tree stump. The Aldens had seen these kids arguing before, but never quite like this. David and Zack seemed to be playing tug-of-war with a metal box.

"What's going on?" Henry called out to them.

Zack, Zoe, and David all froze as the Aldens got off their bikes and ran over to them.

"They're trying to steal this cache," David said as he yanked the metal box out of Zack's grip once and for all. "They've been stealing caches all over town. But I'm not going to let them steal this one." He held the metal box tight against his chest.

"Wait a minute," Jessie said, turning to the Zeller twins. "You two have been stealing the caches?" The Aldens had been pretty sure the thief wasn't the Zellers or the Greenes.

"No!" Zoe said, clearly insulted. "We just told David—we're not stealing them, we're protecting them." She pulled on the box again, but David backed away from her, still holding it tight.

"Protecting them from what?" Henry asked.

"From being stolen by the real thief!" Zack cried.

"We're only taking caches that have travel bugs in them," Zoe explained.

"Why?" Benny asked.

"Some of these travel bugs have been traveling a long time," Zack said. "And some of them have come from really far away. Like Europe. So we don't want the thief to get them."

"One of the caches we took has a flag from Switzerland that has already traveled around the world three times."

Zack nodded. "We've got another one that has a racing car that belonged to a little boy in California," Zack added. "It was one of his favorite cars, but he turned it into a travel bug so he could watch it travel around the country. Think how he'd feel if he found out the cache his car was in got stolen!"

"Let me get this straight," David said. "You guys didn't take any of the first caches that went missing. You've only taken the last few. And you're only taking ones with travel bugs in them?"

"That's right," Zoe said. "And we're leaving notes for the real thief that say 'ha ha!' As in 'ha-ha, you didn't get this one!'" She held up a note just like the one Andy had found.

"We've kept track of where all the caches we took are supposed to go," Zack said. "Once the thief goes away, we'll put them back. But not until we're sure they'll be safe."

"Is that what you were talking about when we saw you in the woods after the geocaching meeting?" Jessie asked. "You said something like 'maybe we should put them back.' Were you talking about the caches you'd taken?"

"Yes," Zack said. "Zoe thought we should take the treasure out and put the empty boxes back where we found them. But I thought it would be hard to keep track of what belonged in which box if we did that."

"That *would* be hard to keep track of," Violet agreed.

"We started gathering up caches with travel bugs in them last weekend," Zoe said. "In case you were wondering what we were doing behind the mall that day you saw us back there."

"I sure wish we knew who took all those other caches," David said.

"So do we," Zoe said. "Our dad's been talking to a lot of people in the geocaching club. If the real thief isn't caught soon, we're probably going to disband the club."

"My dad said the same thing," David said. Nobody wants to keep the club going if somebody's going to steal all our caches."

"Then we're going to have to work hard to find the real thief before the club disbands," Violet said.

"Well, we know something about the missing caches," Benny announced. "They were all hidden by the same person!"

Zack, Zoe, and David all turned to Benny.

"They were?" David asked. "That's interesting."

"Who hid them?" Zack and Zoe asked.

"Cal Edwards," Violet replied.

Zack and Zoe's eyes widened. "And he's missing, too!" Zoe exclaimed.

"Actually, he's not," Henry said. "He got called out of town suddenly to take care of his mother."

The Aldens told the other kids about their visit to Cal's house and about their conversation with Mrs. Michaelson.

"Well, I'm sorry about Cal's mother, but I'm glad he's okay," David said.

"So are we," Zack and Zoe said.

The Aldens were happy to see the Zellers and the Greenes agreeing on something. Maybe they could all work together now and find the missing cache?

"One thing we can tell you about Cal—his caches are more fun to find than anyone's," Zoe said with a smile.

"That's true," David agreed, smiling back.

"Why?" Violet asked. "Why are his caches more fun than anyone else's?"

"I think he puts more time into them than other people do," Zack said. "He puts them in really interesting containers. For instance, there was one he made out of a piece of plumbing pipe."

"And there was that other one that was part of a Halloween decoration," Zoe put in.

"Oh, that's a great one!" David laughed. "That's the 'Halloween Horror' cache," he told the Aldens. "You guys should try and find that one. You'll love it!"

"He also hides the containers in really interesting places and he always has the best trade items," Zack said.

"Yeah, once we found a Chinese kite in one of his new caches," Zoe said. "We were the first to find that one."

"We found a twenty-dollar bill in one of the ones that we were first to find," David said.

"It's strange that all the missing caches

were Cal's," Zack said.

"Unless Cal took them himself," Benny said.

Everyone stopped to stare at the youngest Alden.

"But why would he do that?" Zoe asked. "He knows everyone loves to hunt for his caches."

"Well, maybe he didn't mean to keep them so long," Benny said. "Maybe he meant to put them back, but he didn't have a chance to put them back before he left town."

"But why would he take them in the first place, Benny?" Henry asked. "That's the one thing we still don't know."

Benny sighed. "And it's a big thing."

* * * *

Violet could hear Jessie tossing and turning in the other bed in their room, but the room was still dark. Watch was asleep on the floor between them. Violet could hear him snoring. She wished she were snoring.

"Jessie?" she whispered, "What are you doing?"

"I can't sleep. I thought I'd get a glass of milk," Jessie said.

"I can't sleep, either. Maybe I'll get a glass of milk, too."

The two of them tiptoed out into the hallway. Watch padded behind them.

"Hey, there's a light on downstairs," Violet whispered.

The light was coming from the direction of the family room.

"I wonder who else is up?" Jessie whispered back.

The girls crept down the stairs. But rather than head for the kitchen, they turned toward the family room.

"Henry!" Jessie whispered. "What are you doing up?"

Henry was sitting at the computer. His notebook lay open in front of him.

"I couldn't sleep," he said. "I can't stop thinking about those missing caches. There has to be something we're just not seeing."

Just then Benny wandered sleepily into the room. "What's everyone doing?" he asked out loud.

The others jumped in surprise.

"Benny!" Jessie said. "What are you doing out of bed at this hour?"

"I wanted to find out what you guys were doing out of bed at this hour," he replied.

Violet smiled. "I guess none of us could sleep."

"We're all worried about the geocaching club," Jessie said. She, Violet, and Benny sat down on the couch.

Henry nodded. "I would hate to see it disband."

"Especially before Cal gets back," Violet said.

"Too bad Cal isn't here to fix everything," Benny said, resting his head against Violet's shoulder.

"Wait a minute," Jessie said, sitting up a little straighter. "That's it! Cal was fixing something right before he left. Remember?"

The others looked confused.

"What does that have to do with anything, Jessie?" Violet asked. "We don't even know what Cal was fixing."

"Well, what if he was fixing some damaged cache boxes?" Jessie asked, her eyes dancing with excitement.

"Then maybe Benny's theory was correct," Henry said.

Benny was still confused. "What theory?" he asked. "And what *is* a theory, anyway?"

"A theory is an idea you have to explain something," Violet said. "But you don't know for sure you're right."

"Oh." Benny nodded. Then he wrinkled his nose. "What was my theory again?"

"You wondered if Cal had taken the caches," Henry reminded Benny. "You said maybe he didn't mean to take them for long, but he got called away before he could put them back."

"The only thing wrong with your theory was it didn't explain *why* he took them in the first place," Jessie said. "But if Cal took them because they needed some repair work, then that would explain everything."

"Is there any way to test this theory?" Violet asked.

"We could go online and see if there are any comments about damaged caches," Henry suggested.

"Good idea, Henry," Jessie said. Henry turned his chair back around so he was facing the computer. The others gathered around as he logged into geocaching.com.

Henry pulled up the web page for the first missing cache, then scrolled down to the list of comments.

"Yup. That one says the container is coming apart," Violet said, pointing to the second comment from the top.

Henry went to the next cache on their list and read the third comment out loud. "'Great hide! No trade items in container. No log book, either.'"

"Isn't it possible Cal would've taken that one, too, just to fill it with things to trade again?" Violet asked.

"It's possible," Jessie agreed.

The Aldens checked the listings for the other missing caches. All had reports of damage or missing trade items.

"So maybe my theory is right!" Benny said.

"Maybe," Henry said. "We won't know for sure until Cal comes back."

"But what if the geocaching club shuts down before that?" Violet said.

"We'll just have to convince them to stay together," Jessie said.

CHAPTER 10

The Truth Comes Out

The Greenfield Geocachers Club met again that Friday. Once again, the nature center was closed and the club members were gathered out front when the Aldens arrived.

The Robertsons were back from visiting Andy's grandmother, but the Aldens didn't have a chance to chat with them. Everyone was talking about shutting down the geocaching club.

"How can we shut down without Cal?" one of the college students asked.

"Well, we don't know where he is or when he'll be back," another college student responded.

"We can't go on like this," the man in the blue jacket said. "Several of us were out geocaching yesterday and we discovered several caches that were there last weekend are missing now."

"Yes. Instead of finding caches, we found notes that said, 'ha ha!'" the lady next to him said with a frown.

"I don't think we have any choice but to shut down," said the man beside her.

"Wait!" Benny interrupted. "Don't do that!"

"Cal's not missing," Violet said.

"And we're the ones who left the notes that said 'ha-ha!'" Zoe spoke up.

The Aldens told everyone what they knew about Cal, and the Zeller twins explained why they took some of the caches and replaced them with notes that said "ha-ha."

"Okay, but what about the other missing caches?" Mr. Robertson asked. "The ones the Zellers didn't take?"

"We have a theory about that," Benny said. Benny liked the word *theory* now.

"What's your theory?" Andy asked.

"We think Cal took them!" Benny said.

"What?" Mr. Zeller asked with disbelief. Mr. and Mrs. Greene shook their heads.

"Why would he do such a thing?" Mrs. Greene muttered.

"Because they were his to begin with," Henry explained. "If you look up all the missing caches on geocaching.com, you'll see that they all had some kind of damage."

"Or they needed to be refilled with new things to trade," Jessie added.

Henry continued. "We think Cal went around and took the caches so he could repair them. But then, before he could put them all back, he got called out of town."

"That's a very interesting theory!" said a voice behind them.

Everyone turned toward the voice.

"Cal!" the Aldens cried.

Cal carried a bulging black garbage bag. It looked like the same bag he'd been

carrying in the dog park.

The whole group ran to him and shook his hand or patted him on the back.

"We're glad you're okay. How is your mother?" someone asked him.

"She's much better, thanks," Cal said. "I'm sorry you were all so worried. And I'm sorry the nature center has been closed all this time. I wish I had taken the time to leave a key with one of my volunteers, but at the time all I could think about was getting to the airport."

"That's okay," Mr. Robertson said. "We understand."

"And I should have called one of you to let you know what was happening," Cal went on. "But I'm afraid I didn't think to make phone calls until my mother started to get better. I was too worried about her. I didn't even think to bring my cell phone with me."

"We're just glad you're back, Cal," Andy said.

"Thanks, everyone," Cal said, smiling. Then he reached into his pocket, pulled out a key, and unlocked the nature center.

Everyone went inside.

"So, what about my theory?" Benny asked Cal, once everyone was settled. "Was I right? Did you take the caches?"

"Yes, I did," Cal replied. "And it was just like you said. I saw there were problems with several of my caches, so I gathered them up that day I saw you kids at the dog park."

Cal opened the garbage bag and took out some metal boxes, covered pails, and other containers. He set them all on the table in front of him.

"So you weren't collecting garbage like we thought," Violet said. "You were collecting caches!"

"That's right," Cal said. "In fact, I was going to tell you what I was doing and ask you if you knew what geocaching was. But then I got that phone call about my mother. I'm glad you kids found out about geocaching on your own."

"We ran into Andy and his dad just a few minutes after we left you," Benny said. "They told us all about it."

"And you thought we were stealing all the caches just to prevent your family from winning the contest," Zoe told David Greene.

"I did," David admitted. "I'm sorry about that. But I bet you thought I was doing the same thing. I bet you thought I was trying to prevent you from winning the contest."

"We're sorry, too," Zack said.

"Speaking of contests," Mr. Robertson said, holding up his hands. He held a computer printout in one hand and a GPS box in the other. "Yesterday was the last day of the month."

"So the contest is over?" David said.

"Do we have a winner?" Zoe asked expectantly. "Do we know who wins the new GPS?"

Mr. Robertson scratched his chin. "Well, there's a slight problem with that," he said. "It seems we have a tie. The Green Lights and the Zees both found eighty-three caches this month."

Everyone clapped for the Greenes and the Zellers.

"Great job, all of you," Mr. Robertson said. "But I don't know how we can split this GPS in two."

"I have an idea," Zack said. "We already have a pretty nice GPS. And I'll bet the Greenes do, too."

All three members of the Greene family nodded.

"I think we should give the new GPS to the Aldens to thank them for solving the mystery of the missing caches," Zack said.

The Aldens were stunned.

"That's a great idea," David said.

Everyone else nodded and started clapping again.

Cal nudged Benny. "Go get your new GPS, kids," he said.

So the Aldens went over to Mr. Robertson and he handed Henry the box with the GPS.

"Wow, thanks!" Henry said.

"Thank *you* for solving the mystery," Mr. Robertson said.

Cal nodded toward the table full of

geocache containers. "I've fixed these caches," he said. "So I could use some help putting them back in their hiding places this afternoon."

"Sure." "Of course." "We'd love to help!" everyone said.

"It looks like the geocaching club will stay together after all," Violet said.

"Hooray!" Benny said.

* * * *

The next weekend, the Aldens took out a large square plastic container with a tight-fitting lid. They set it on the kitchen table and Grandfather and Mrs. MacGregor helped the children decide what to buy for the container. Jessie wrote down all their ideas.

"Well, we definitely need a log book and pencil," Henry said.

"And plastic bags that zip closed so the stuff doesn't get damaged," Jessie added.

"How about a compass and a water bottle?" Grandfather suggested.

"I've got some toys from fast food meals that we could put in there," Benny said.

"Some people include a disposable camera so that people can take pictures of themselves finding the cache," Violet said.

"That would be fun," Henry said. "Then we could upload the pictures to the website."

"Could I make some chocolate chip cookies?" Mrs. MacGregor asked. "People who are hunting for treasure in the woods are probably hungry."

"Yes, but you're not supposed to put food in a cache," Jessie pointed out. "Even though it's sealed up, animals have a strong sense of smell."

"She could put her chocolate chip cookie recipe on a card and we could leave that in the cache," Violet said.

"That's a great idea," Benny said. "Anybody would be lucky to find Mrs. MacGregor's chocolate chip cookie recipe!"

"Why thank you, Benny," Mrs. MacGregor said. "In that case, maybe you'd like to help me bake some cookies this afternoon?"

"I would!" Benny cried. "I really would!"

Grandfather took the children shopping for the items on Jessie's list. When they got home they packed everything in the big container, then went outside.

"So where should we hide our cache?" Jessie asked.

"I've got a perfect idea," Violet said. "Follow me!" She led them around to the backyard.

"I know where Violet's taking us!" Benny cried. "To our boxcar!"

"That's right, Benny," Violet said.

The children walked around inside and outside the boxcar, searching for the perfect hiding place. The settled on a spot of tall grass just behind one of the back wheels.

Benny slid the container behind the wheel and the others gathered a few rocks and sticks to pile up all around it.

"Now all we have to do is use our GPS to figure out the coordinates and then enter our new cache at geocaching.com," Jessie said.

"What are we going to call our cache?" Henry asked. "Any ideas?"

"How about 'All's Well That Ends Well?'" said Violet.